DAVEY PANDA

Can Do All Things Through Christ

JUNE 15, 2020
MYRA G. LOVE MINISTRIES

Myra G. Love Ministries

Myracar7er@gmail.com

Copyright © 2020 Author Myra G. Love

All rights reserved. This book or any portion thereof may not be reproduced or used in any manner whatsoever without the express written permission of the publisher except for the use of brief quotations in a book review. Author/Writer has freedom of speech and is protected by the 1st Amendment of the United States Constitution. This book is Fictional Religion and Christian Based!

ISBN 978-0-578-71805-7

Davey asked, "Mamma, may I please go outside to play?"

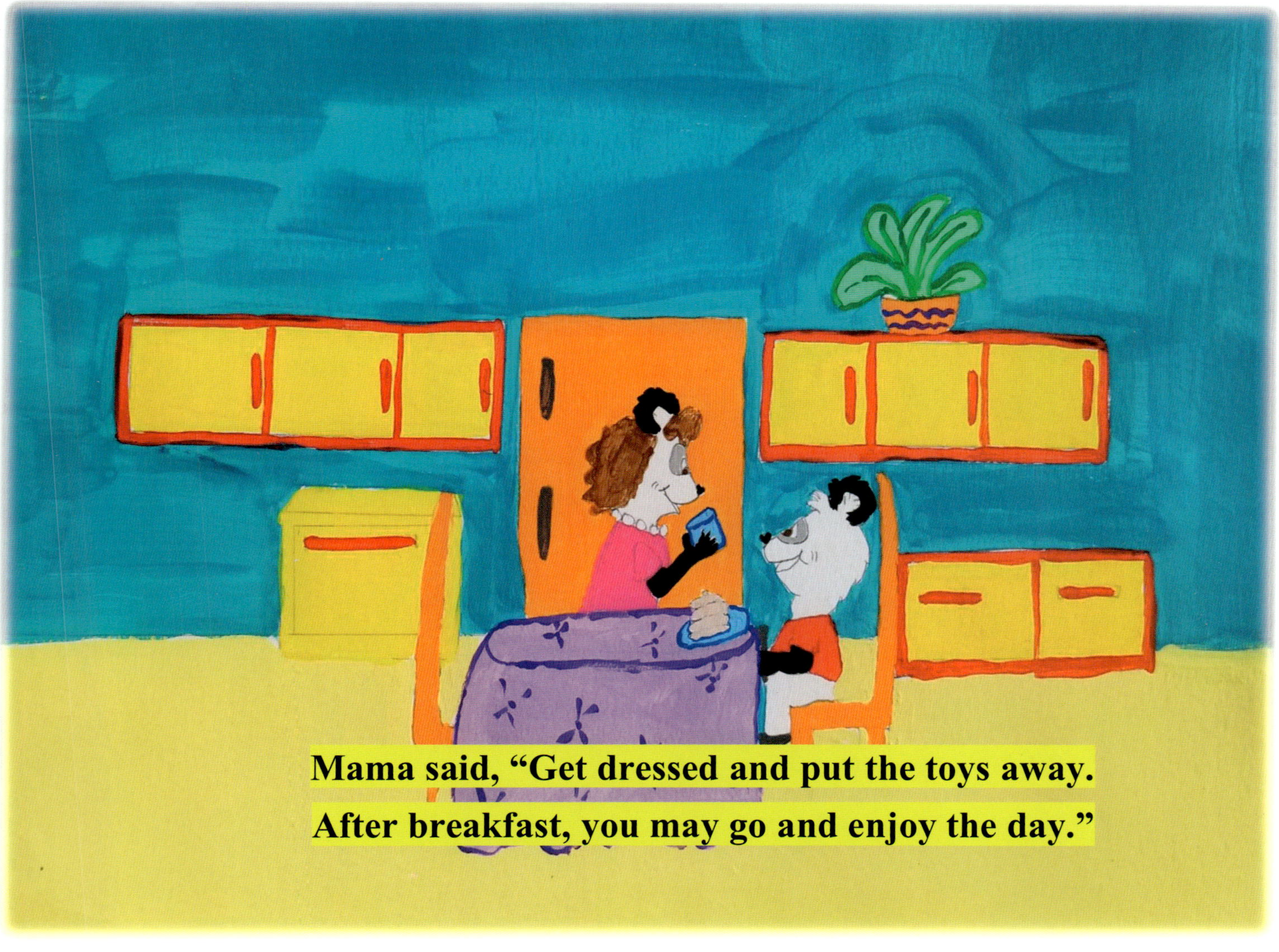

Mama said, "Get dressed and put the toys away.
After breakfast, you may go and enjoy the day."

Mama said, "Yes be careful because you have to learn to ride."

Davey wanted to ride, like all of his friends.
He fell off the bike again, again and again.

It was bedtime. He prayed, "Lord help me learn to ride my bike?"

Papa took the day off, to show Davey how to ride.
Papa said, "Hold the handle bars and peddle, I'll be right by your side."

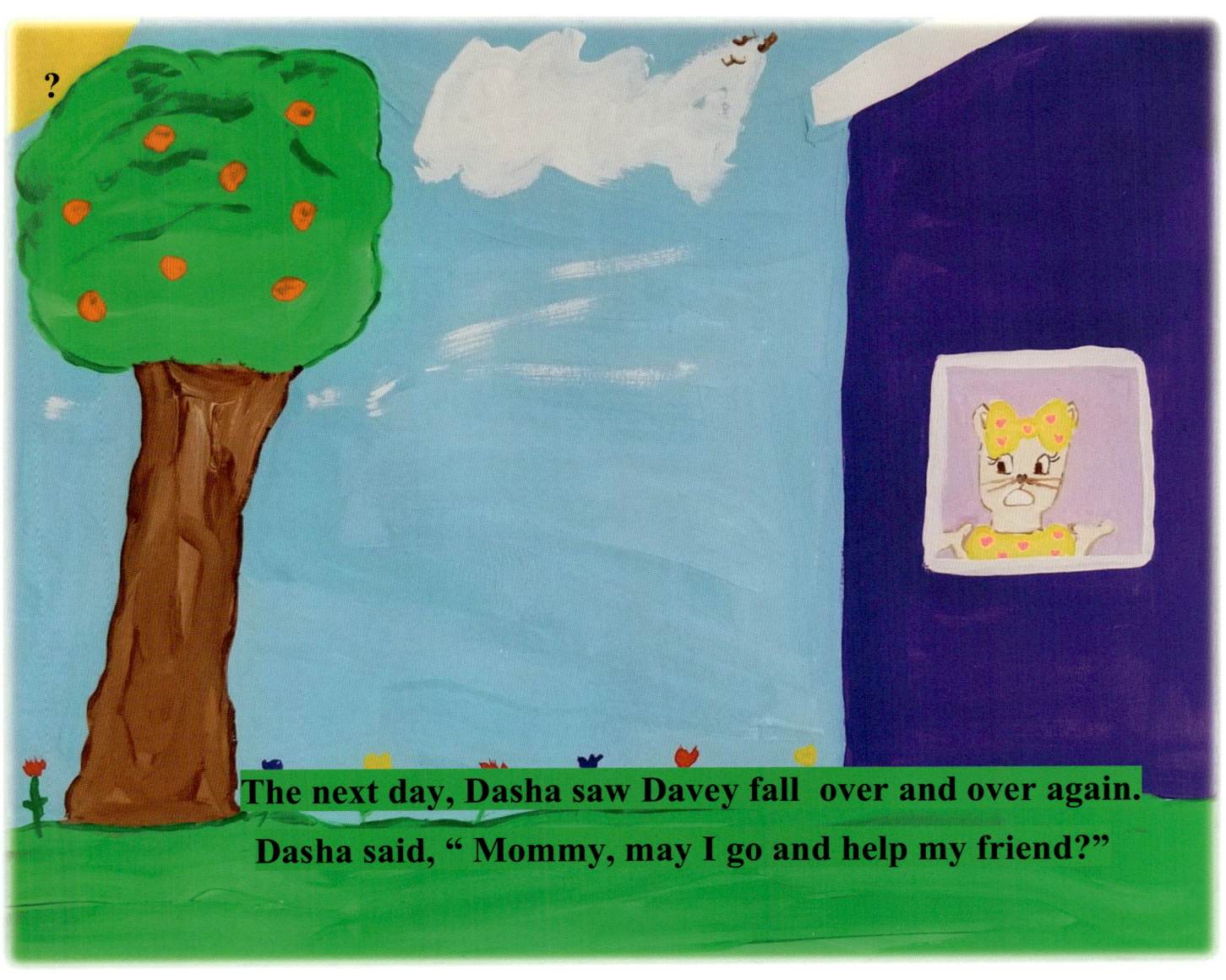

The next day, Dasha saw Davey fall over and over again. Dasha said, " Mommy, may I go and help my friend?"

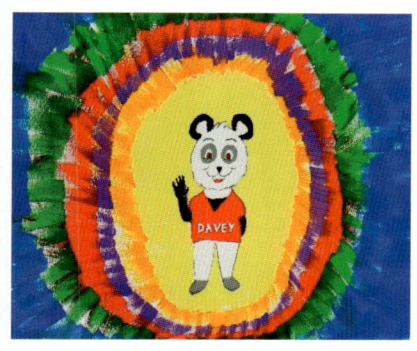

Davey's Corner

1. What did Davey have a hard time doing?
2. Why was Davey sad?
3. What did Davey see his friends doing?
4. What did Dasha say to help Davey?
5. What was your favorite part of the book?
6. What do You have a hard time doing?

Davey says:

Philippians 4:13 I can do all things through Christ who strengthens me.

Draw Something for Davey or Dasha Below

Draw Davey or Dasha Below

This book is dedicated to the Lord Jesus.

A Special thank you to all of my wonderful supporters.

May the Lord Bless you all now and forevermore!